WELCOME TO LIFE

by Dan Lietha
Foreword by Ken Ham

Answers in Genesis
www.AnswersInGenesis.org

First printing: September 2003

ISBN: 1-893345-15-7

Printed in the United States of America

This book is dedicated
to my parents,
Duane & Helen Lietha.

Thanks for your love and support.

Table of Contents

Foreword

There are many ways to communicate, but I've discovered that cartoons are one of the most effective ways to communicate both simple and complex concepts, especially the central issues of creation/evolution and the Book of Genesis.

'A picture is worth a thousand words,' the saying goes. And it is not easy to take 'a thousand words' and turn them into one picture. However, my friend and colleague Dan Lietha has been endowed by His Creator with unique gifts and talents to be able to do just that.

Not only is Dan a superb cartoonist and illustrator, but he also has the ability to take numerous concepts from creationist books and lectures, and turn them into illustrations and cartoons that communicate in both a serious and humorous way. Not only will you immensely enjoy looking at his cartoons, but you will also learn biblical, scientific and philosophical concepts that you will never forget and that will help you in challenging others to believe the truth of God's Word.

So prepare yourself for a journey through time—from Eden to the present. You will laugh, cry, be challenged, educated and convicted. Most of all, you will learn those eternal truths that so many in this world need to hear.

Buckle up for the trip of a lifetime. You will never think the same way about life again after reading this collection, a unique contribution to creation apologetic resources.

Ken Ham
Founder and President
Answers in Genesis–USA

The creation of *After Eden*

Back in 1999, the *Answers in Genesis* website, www.AnswersInGenesis.org, was really taking off by leaps and bounds, and I wanted to help increase traffic to the site. My burden was (and still is) to get as many people as possible to discover the vital biblical and scientific information that AiG's website provides.

In thinking about the best vehicle for increasing our web traffic, I made two important observations.

1. People with access to the internet like to email their friends things that amuse them and information that they want others to see.

2. Other websites were successfully using cartoons as a way to generate large amounts of web traffic.

I thought AiG could produce a cartoon feature to attract viewers as well.

So in late 1999, the first *After Eden* cartoon appeared on the AiG website, along with an announcement that a new weekly cartoon feature would be launched on the first Monday of January 2000.

Since then, thousands of people have viewed and used the *After Eden* cartoons. *After Eden* is used on lots of other websites, too, which point back to the AiG site. The cartoon is emailed all over the world each day and printed in many church newsletters. Praise the Lord for all the people who have joined us in spreading the word about *Answers in Genesis* by sharing these funny little cartoons!

At the beginning of each chapter, you will find a behind-the-scenes look at the *After Eden* cartoons (how they're made, reader responses, etc.). It is my hope that these bits of information will make the *After Eden* cartoons more enjoyable and will encourage and challenge cartoon fans and artists alike.

Chapter 1
ADAM & EVE

We are all here because of them—in more ways than one.

First signs of life in the universe

In the beginning, EVERYBODY was a creationist!

The actual First World War

Adam & Eve would often reminisce
about the '*very good*' old days.

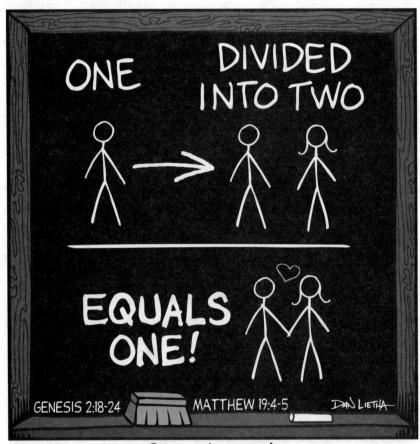

Genesis math

Adam & Eve think back to what they did
wrong in the Garden of Eden.

In the days before gossip
was possible.

It suddenly became apparent to Adam
that he could probably be more effective
in his role as head of the marriage.

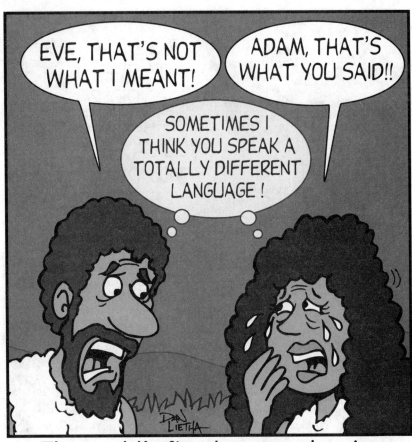

The world's first language barrier problems actually came much earlier than the Tower of Babel.

Adam greets his wife after a long day of
working 'by the sweat of his brow.' Eve
immediately detects more than just
his brow was sweating!

The earth's first 'Ice Age.'

Adam's 'surprise bouquet of roses' was a sweet idea, but he forgot to remind Eve about this new thing called '**thorns.**'

Drawing lots of plants is the key for presenting 'pre-Fall world' art to a 'post-Fall world' audience!

'How could Adam & Eve be in their
''birthday suits''
when they were never born?'

Genesis 1, creation day 6.
The real 'Walking with Dinosaurs' we'd
like to see on the Discovery Channel!

The birth of a cartoon

As I put this book together, my wife and I are expecting our first child; and yes, this exciting event hasn't gone untouched by my cartooning. On 24 February 2003, I posted the cartoon below on the *After Eden* website—a few weeks before my wife and I made the official announcement.

I received many emails complimenting the message in the cartoon, but no comments about any possible hidden meaning. Because my co-workers had made comments about my previous baby cartoons (see page 23), I expected at least some speculation.

After we made our baby news public, several co-workers admitted that they had suspected something when they saw the cartoon, but they were afraid it might be nothing more than just another baby cartoon. This time, however, the cartoon was inspired by a real baby!

By the way, my wife and I still don't know our daughter's name.

Isaiah 43:1
> But now, thus says the LORD, your Creator, O Jacob,
> And He who formed you, O Israel,
> 'Do not fear, for I have redeemed you;
> I have called you by name; you are Mine!'

Chapter 2

Be fruitful
and multiply

The world's first parents

In the beginning, the title of 'mother' was first given to one of these two choices. Do you know which one?

Eve   Earth

Hint: The earth is not your mother.

And Adam called his wife's name Eve; because she was [to be] the mother of all living. Genesis 3:20

As new parents, Adam & Eve learned
to have different expectations
for their children.

Back then, the answer to 'that question' was: 1. Created from the dust of the ground 2. Made from a man's side 3. From a husband and a wife.

Not only was Eve 'mother of ALL the living,' there were many, many days she certainly FELT like it!

Adam & Eve were the very first parents
to be embarrassed about the kind of
clothes they wore in their younger days.

Eve gets an easy question.

The first man, Adam, could encourage
singles like no-one else in all of history!

Adam and Eve's kids talk about
the age of the earth.

Then the days of Adam after he became the father of Seth were eight hundred years, and he had **other sons and daughters.** Genesis 5:4

A DAY IN THE LIFE OF THE MOTHER OF ALL THE LIVING!
STOP PUSHING!
HA HA HA
URP!
MINE!
MINE!
MINE!
MINE!

The REAL part of *After Eden*

Aside from a few mild instances of 'creative license' (see page 132), *After Eden* is as true-to-reality as I can make it. Here are a few things that I drew to reflect the true history of the universe, as taught in Genesis:

- Dinosaurs and man living together (pages 16, 49, 51). Since all land animals (dinosaurs are land animals) and man were created on day 6 of the creation week, we know that dinosaurs and people lived at the same time.

- Adam and Eve's skin shade. Many times, Adam and Eve are pictured as two blonde, light-skinned people in the Garden of Eden. However, genetically speaking, it makes more sense that their skin wasn't 'too light or too dark.' In *After Eden* they are pictured as 'middle brown'—this is the best starting point for the wide range of skin shades that we see in the world today.

- Noah's Ark. This amazing vessel is a common source of distortion by cartoonists. The Ark in *After Eden* is based on the biblical description given in Genesis 6:14-16.

- The pre-Flood earth has only one continent (see pages 4 & 22). This is an instance where I knew some people might be confused by an earth that looks different from the modern earth, but I believe this is the correct way to portray it. The continent most likely split up during Noah's Flood, resulting in the various landmasses we see today.

- Dinosaurs going into the Ark (page 49). When showing animals boarding the Ark, it seems to be standard practice to show only animals that are living today. My cartoons include dinosaurs among the animals that found safety on the Ark. Notice that they are not the full-grown dinosaurs but younger (and therefore smaller) ones that would have no problem fitting onto the Ark (see pages 78, 79).

Chapter 3

Cain's wife

A short chapter dedicated to the most famous
nameless person in history.

A historic moment in earth history as
Cain's young son becomes the first
to ask about where Cain got his wife.

Some people just never expect to get
the answer to THAT question!

The look of *After Eden*—
The *A is for Adam*/*After Eden* connection

In 1995, I illustrated the children's book *A is for Adam*. That book has had a big impact on the way I continue to draw scenes from the Book of Genesis.

- Adam and Eve—You may notice that Adam and Eve don't look quite the same throughout this book. I started *After Eden* by drawing them with a loose, 'cartoony' style (see pages 3, 42, 43). As time went on, I adopted a look similar to the one I gave them in *A is for Adam*.

- Adam and Eve's clothing—In *A is for Adam*, Adam and Eve are clothed with the skin of a slain lamb. The thought behind this is that God killed and shed the blood of an animal—possibly a lamb—to provide a covering for the sin of Adam and Eve. This covering is a picture of the sacrifice that Christ would make as the Lamb of God who provided a final covering for the sin of the world. I incorporated this thought into *After Eden*, so that Adam and Eve are wearing white lambskin clothes while everyone else has colored clothing.

- The look of the forbidden fruit—Since the Bible does not specify what kind of fruit was 'forbidden' (we don't believe it was an apple), I 'invented' a forbidden fruit for *A is for Adam*. It's sort of a giant berry-plum type of thing (Ken Ham says it looks like a hand grenade, since that's the effect it had). This is another element I carried over into *After Eden*.

- A couple of other *Answers in Genesis* publications have made their way into *After Eden*. An AiG dinosaur tract can be seen on page 149, and an actual issue of *Creation* magazine can be seen on page 82.

Chapter 4

After Eden
in living
color

Cartoonists didn't evolve.

God just created them funny!

—Dan Lietha

The future population of earth
appeared doubtful for quite a
while, until Adam & Eve finally
kissed and made up.

Adjusting from paradise to life in a cursed world, Adam & Eve would often update each other with new discoveries.

In his first attempt to be romantic,
Adam merely states the obvious.

In the beginning, anything done for the first time was a **'new world record.'**

Eve discovers sarcasm.

Adam & Eve in their later years.

Methuselah on New Year's Day.

'Oh, we won't need life preservers on the Ark. The Ark IS the life preserver!'

The undocumented first use of this
well-known phrase.

In the Book of Job, God told Job to
'behold behemoth' (Job 40:15-24).
It was probably also a good idea to
BEWARE BEHEMOTH!

'Mom, I think Dad is taking the "day of rest" a little too far.'

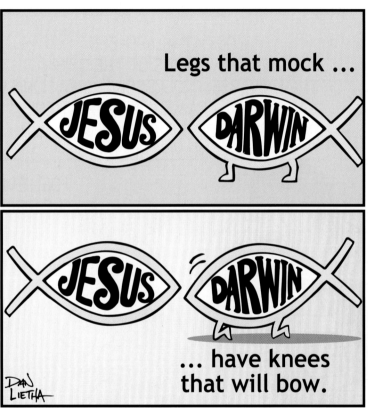

At the name of Jesus EVERY KNEE WILL
BOW ... and every tongue will confess
that Jesus Christ is Lord.
Philippians 2:10a,11a

When pigs fly ...

'Tell me again why I should trust scientists' ability to be accurate about life on Earth **"millions of years"** ago ...'

'Have you ever noticed that in most evolutionary films, the primitive humans are less intelligent than the animals they supposedly outlived?'

1 Peter 1:24-25

'... and this new discovery completely changes everything you were ever taught about the origin of life. Oh, wait! A newer discovery totally changes what I just reported ...'

Little Edmund had to keep reminding himself that broccoli was originally created 'very good.'

Be angry, and yet do not sin; do not let
the sun go down on your anger.
Ephesians 4:26

Beauty (and humor) is in the eye of the biased

Isn't it funny how two people can view the same thing and have completely different reactions to it? This is the case with the 'Accurate Science?' cartoon (see page 58). Several *After Eden* readers, whose views on biblical and scientific matters are different from mine, were really upset when they saw this weather-related cartoon.

I've collected quite a few emails similar to this one:

'That is ludicrous propaganda. The weather man is more sophisticated than this. With the new GPS systems going into effect, the weather predictions will be marvelously closer than they already are. You can't tell me meteorologists make this mistake often when, in fact, they rarely do, but I'm talking to someone who likely believes in just going outside to see what the weather is "right now" and ignores what valid resources have to say about what it will become in the near and distant future.'

Some months after the 'Accurate Science?' cartoon appeared on the web, it was printed in the *Answers in Genesis* newsletter. I then received this email:

Dear Dan,

That is a great cartoon on page 18 of the *Answers Update*. I would like to use that cartoon, if you don't mind, when I talk for AiG, since it works into my 30 years as a weather forecaster.

Thanks,
Mike Oard
meteorologist

It's encouraging to know that, even if some people think I don't have a clue, a meteorologist with 30 years experience appreciates my cartoon. I don't remember what the weather was like outside my office on the day Mike Oard's email arrived, but I do know it was pretty sunny inside my office!

Chapter 5

Beyond Genesis 5:5

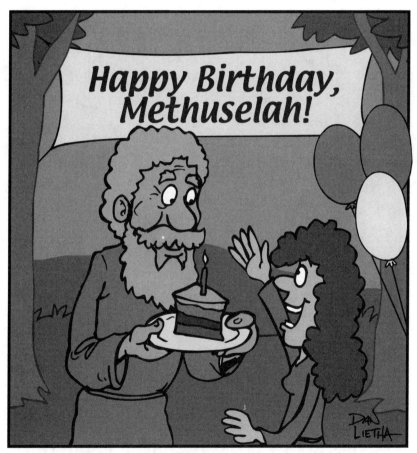

'480 years old! How does it feel to be middle aged?'

Methuselah's great grandson knew this
was going to take a while.

Job hunting in the days before
Noah's Flood.

One advantage Adam & Eve's children had was **never** having to listen to their parents complain about a difficult childhood.

Those believing Adam & Eve to be a
myth were not encouraged.

George is thankful for a son who not only honors his father, but also pays attention even when the family Bible reading goes through the genealogies.

To err is human ...

The people who read my cartoons are more than just passive readers—they are also reviewers. Their comments help me to produce better artwork.

A reader once pointed out that I had drawn a belly button on Eve. OOPS! Most likely, neither Adam nor Eve would have had belly buttons (which result from umbilical cords) because neither of them was in a mother's womb! I quickly performed a 'belly-button-ectomy' to correct the mistake.

Not all of the critiques require changes in my cartoons. Here are a couple of my 'favorite' examples:

Critique of the cartoon on page 37: **'People do not faint because of apologetics.'**

When I read this, the thought came to my mind: 'Sure people do. It happens in cartoons all the time!'

Critique of the cartoon on page 3: **'At the beginning of human life/civilization, it is unlikely that any human was a Biblical Creationist as the Bible did not exist.'**

Actually, Adam & Eve *did* have God's Word because He spoke to them directly!

Another concern was raised about the book *A is for Adam,* which I illustrated with a style similar to *After Eden.* This person was well meaning and genuinely concerned, but his concern about Adam's nose still made me chuckle:

'I was taken aback when I saw the size of Adam's nose, in the book, A IS FOR ADAM. This, you might think, is only a trifle, but since God said, "Let us make man in our image," why does Adam have to have an oversized nose? I think it's disrespectful to God.'

But what if Adam really did have a big nose?

Chapter 6

Noah's

Flood

And only Noah was left, together with those that were with him in the ark. Gen 7:23b

Even the largest full-grown creatures
were once small!

Baby dinosaurs fit into 'small' eggs.
Juvenile dinosaurs fit on a HUGE Ark!

Genesis 9:15

Dan Lietha

The 'great baptismal malfunction of 2002' was the event that made Pastor Tim realize it had to be a GLOBAL flood that God promised He would never send again!

'If Noah's Ark really looked like that,
there wouldn't be anybody alive
today to make those silly arks because
no-one would have survived the Flood.'

'"Part of the earth"? Noah's Flood covered the **entire planet**. Doesn't anybody think in "biblical proportions" anymore?'

Christians and cartoons

Most Christians accept cartoons as a legitimate tool for ministry, but occasionally I hear objections. One pastor made this comment about *After Eden:*

'... they seem to be completely out of keeping with the rest of your work, which is serious, scriptural and greatly needed today.'

This is a portion of my reply:

'Many think cartoons are used only to make fun of and mock the things they portray. I would respectfully disagree. Think of the hundreds of editorial cartoons that were printed in newspapers around the world expressing the tragedy, pain and loss in the terrorist attacks of September 11, 2001. These illustrations were cartoons, and their purpose wasn't to mock or show disrespect but to honor and mourn the dead and injured victims—a very serious thing.'

After Eden is intended to be humorous, but it also deals with some very serious topics. My intent is not to mock or make light of these topics, but to make the reader think about them in a biblical way. Here are a few serious topics:

* Sin and its effect on human relationships and marriage
* The intrusion of death into this world
* Physical pain and sickness as the result of the Curse
* The difficulty of parenthood
* People's tendency to listen to man's word and reject God's Word
* The true cause of this cursed world—man's sin
* The death of a friend

My heart as a Christian cartoonist is to effectively communicate a biblical message to everyone who sees these images. Cartoons are a very effective communication tool, and we find in the AiG ministry that cartoons can reach people many times faster than words alone.

Chapter 7

Holidays

'Well, our Creator did say,
"Let there be light!"'

If there is an animal in your 'Easter
story' this year, make sure
it's a serpent rather than a bunny.

Where do the ideas come from?

People often ask me where I get the ideas for my cartoons. (Many times, as I sit at my drawing board staring at a blank sheet of paper, I ask myself that same question!) Things that happen around me often spark ideas:

Movies and TV programs

News items

Events on the calendar

(This cartoon was made for Stacia McKeever, co-creator of the *Answers for Kids* section in *Creation* magazine.)

Suggested Ideas

I'd like to thank the following people for their ideas:

Relation ships

Be kind to one another, tender-hearted, forgiving each other, just as God in Christ also has forgiven you.

Ephesians 4:32

The original man and woman had a
perfect understanding of each other.
Sin brought the curse. The curse
brought many books.

Reality weddings

Please handle with care

Some *After Eden* cartoons highlight truths in God's Word, and others challenge alternative ways of thinking that disagree with God's Word.

I know that these 'challenge' cartoons may be offensive—to a degree—to those who do not believe the Bible. My goal, however, is not to be ugly or 'in your face,' but I want to catch people's attention and possibly cause them to think about Scripture in a new way.

In my creation cartooning, I try to stay away from cheap shots against evolutionists and others whose view of Scripture is different from mine. It is easy to misuse images to make 'monkeys' (literally) out of people who believe humans are related to the animal kingdom. You don't have to look hard to find this type of name-calling in various media. I would encourage Christians to avoid this type of imagery. It doesn't produce anything profitable in challenging the thinking of people on 'the other side.'

As Christians set out to challenge the thinking of others, I believe we should strive to do it for the right reasons and in a positive way.

1 Peter 3:15 states: 'But sanctify Christ as Lord in your hearts, always being ready to make a defense to everyone who asks you to give an account for the hope that is in you, yet with gentleness and reverence.'

We should not forget the last part of that verse, 'with gentleness and reverence.'

I want non-Christians to respond to an *After Eden* cartoon, not because I called them a name or made them look stupid, but because I presented the truth and challenged their thinking.

It's not easy, and the boundaries aren't always clear; but a godly 'challenge,' presented with care and tact, can be quite effective in changing our world.

Chapter 9

The battle of beliefs

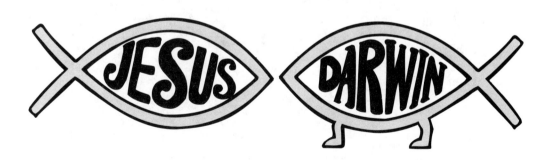

More than just fighting fish

'As anti-creation as most evolutionists are, they are some of the most creative people around.'

Therefore if anyone is in Christ, he is a new creature; the old things passed away; behold, new things have come.
2 Corinthians 5:17

'You know the difference between these two chimps? In public school, I can only say ONE of them was made by an intelligent creator.'

'Have you ever noticed if someone calls you a "monkey," it's an insult, but if they say you came from a monkey, that's "science"?'

'I can see why some people would want
to believe they are related to animals.
Animals have more rights today
than humans do.'

'What's so great about that?
I usually get into trouble when I copy
something someone else has made first!'

The people in *After Eden*

Besides the biblical characters, a few other 'real' people appear in *After Eden* from time to time. It's not important to the cartoon that these people are recognizable. I just put them in simply for the fun of it.

One example of a recognizable person is found on page 121. Buddy Davis (AiG dinosaur sculptor, speaker and musician) is the star of this cartoon. He's the guy with the hat. At the time, Buddy was scheduled to have open-heart surgery, and I drew this cartoon as a get-well card for him.

Another person with a familiar face (although it's a loose resemblance) is found in the church congregation scene on page 139. Hint: he's the man that wrote the foreword to this book. Look for the beard.

Some of the other familiar people included in *After Eden* aren't drawn but are alluded to.

Here are a few examples:

Pastor Tim is the name of a former pastor of mine (see page 80).

The jersey of my favorite Minnesota Vikings player can be found on page 79.

A cartoon about the lady who led me to Christ is on page 150. You can find me at my drawing board in this cartoon.

Not every non–Bible character in my cartoons is based on a real person, but some of them are. So the next time you see a character in *After Eden*, you may just wonder who that really is!

Chapter 10

The forbidden fruit

A chapter dedicated to the most famous unknown fruit in history.
No, it wasn't an apple!

Sally was sure that **IF** there had been
forbidden **VEGETABLES** in the Garden
of Eden instead of forbidden fruit,
Adam & Eve wouldn't have eaten them.

Jim's Grandmother reminds people of the Garden of Eden/Christmas connection by giving out what she calls her 'forbidden fruit cake.'

The making of an ideal Genesis
'teachable moment.'

After Eden: A perspective on life

After Eden is much more than just the title of a cartoon. It's a biblical perspective on the world we live in.

This present world of pain and suffering has caused many people to ask 'WHY?' 'Why is the world this way?' 'Why did this have to happen to my loved one?' 'Why me?'

We must never forget that the search for an answer begins by looking at our place in history. 'We live AFTER Eden—in a post-perfect world. Pain and suffering are a 'normal' part of this world.

Is it God's fault? No. It was our sin (in Adam) that ruined this once-perfect creation. Romans 5:12 teaches: 'Therefore, just as through one man sin entered into the world, and death through sin, and so death spread to all men, because all sinned.'

This side of heaven, we may not know all the specific reasons for the sad situations we face, but the answer begins with the fact that we now live in a sin-cursed world.

So don't be surprised by hard times in your life. After all, we don't live in Eden any more.

Chapter 11

Living in a cursed world

'Because you have done this ...' Genesis 3:14

A lot has changed since Eden,
including opossums.

Before 6 am, George is more inclined to
see each new day as 24 more hours in
a sin-cursed world.

This world has changed since the
original 'very good.'

Killer dinosaurs

Fossils

High heel shoes

Neckties

Lacking an understanding of sin & the curse, some people credit Satan with creating these things.

Billy learns that no matter how cute you are, the wrong application of correct theology cannot save you.

Isn't it ironic that our health problems
started when our ancestor Adam
ate a piece of fruit?

If anything can go wrong,
it will go wrong.
—Murphy's Law

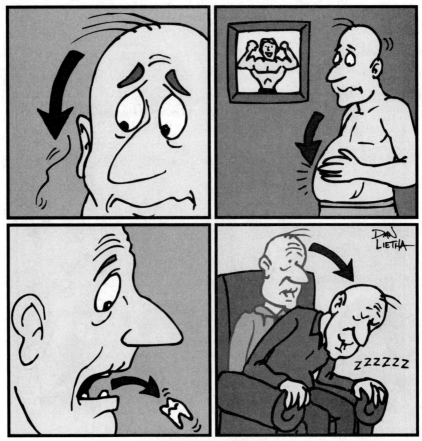

Fallen man

Email from a biblical perspective:
further evidence we live
in a cursed and fallen world!

'Most people wonder why things go wrong. I'm just thankful when anything goes right!'

While a mother-in-law may seem like a curse, the reason people have trouble getting along is because Adam didn't obey the Father of law.

'Yes, man was created in God's image,
regardless of what we see here.'

Creative license

In my *After Eden* cartoons, I strive to portray biblical things, such as Noah's Ark, as accurately as possible (see page 34), but there are times when I intentionally draw things incorrectly. Some instances of 'creative license' are listed below.

- Modern-day road signs during the creation of the universe and in the time of Job (see pages 2 and 51).

- A modern-day life preserver used in Noah's time (page 49).

- Modern-day gravestones for Adam & Eve (page 68).

- A birthday banner, cake, candle and balloons for Methuselah (page 69). I didn't want to show his entire cake—imagine all the candles I'd have to draw!

Why have I made these errors on purpose? Because inserting modern-day objects into a biblical setting can be a very effective way to communicate to a modern audience. Do you get the point in each cartoon?

Also, biblical characters probably would not have said some of the things that I attribute to them, given their culture, but these words get the point across! See pages 8, 12, 29, 31, 36, 42-49 and 69.

On page 28, the children of Adam and Eve refer to their parents by proper names instead of saying father and mother. I couldn't figure out any other way to make this cartoon work! It's important that readers can easily identify Adam and Eve ... Continued on page 142.

Chapter 12

How OLD?

The question of age

'Yes, we are all related to Adam & Eve.
No, Great Grandfather didn't know
them personally!'

How to console some creationists on
one of those 'BIG' birthdays.

When creationists have birthdays.

'To begin our debate, each of you will have one hour to present his point of view. That is a LITERAL hour, just in case one of you would want to interpret it into a longer period of time!'

'Pastor does believe in a "literal 6-day creation," even though his sermons can seem like millions of years.'

For by Him (Jesus) were all things created, that are in heaven, and that are in earth.   Colossians 1:16a

Creative license (continued from page 132)

In using 'creative license,' I believe it's important not to go too far with the biblical text. I realize that this is a gray area, but I'd like to share my opinion.

An example of a biblical truth that cartoonists often alter are the fig leaves worn by Adam and Eve—not what the leaves looked like, but *when* they were worn. This has some important theological implications. The Bible says that Adam and Eve donned fig leaves *immediately after* they sinned, but many cartoonists draw them wearing fig leaves before they sinned or after God clothed them with animal skin.

Cartoonists do this for the simple reason that almost everyone can identify Adam and Eve wearing fig leaves, even without seeing their names. As a visual cue, the fig leaves work well, but this technique violates an important message of Scripture (see Genesis 3:6-11, 21).

In the case of Adam and Eve's appearance before they sinned, I don't suggest that cartoonists just draw them naked! For me, some strategically placed plants work well in those instances (see page 5), and a carefully chosen camera shot can also do the trick (see page 16). In my opinion, if you show Adam and Eve covered *before* their sin, you blur what the Bible teaches about the effects of sin.

There is another potential problem with the clothes that Adam and Eve wore *after* Eden. The Bible says that God gave them coverings of skin to wear—they didn't spend the rest of their lives wearing leaves. If you show Adam and Eve in leaves *after* God supplied this covering of skins, then you detract from the picture of the coming Savior who would shed His blood and become the sacrifice and covering for those who believe in Him (see page 38).

Again, this is my personal approach to biblical cartoons and artwork. I'm not suggesting that this is how everyone should approach these things, but I hope it challenges you to think differently as you view, draw or use biblical images in the future.

Chapter 13

Do you not know? Have you not heard? The Everlasting God, the LORD, the **Creator** of the ends of the earth, does not become weary or tired. His understanding is inscrutable.
Isaiah 40:28

It really bothered Billy that
Amanda was right ... AGAIN!

An *After Eden* family activity

It is my desire that the readers of this book, in addition to enjoying a good laugh, grasp the teaching point behind each cartoon. I'd like to challenge you to look past the pun and find the biblical foundation of the cartoon. (Parents, this could be a fun activity to do with your children!)

Depending on the individual cartoon, you might consider asking what the cartoon teaches about:

- the true history of the universe as taught in the Bible/Genesis
- the true nature of people
- death in this world
- the true origin of humans
- sin and its consequences
- marriage and the family
- pain and suffering
- God's Word versus man's word
- how the world has changed because of sin.

Also, some cartoons contain references to Scripture without mentioning the actual verse. We have reprinted these verses for you in the back of this book (see pages 154-159).

Salva✝ion

For the Son of Man has come to seek and
to save that which was lost. Luke 19:10

Romans 3:23

'The creation ministry is exciting! I've
seen dinosaur tracts used to lead
people to Christ!'

For the word of God is living and active and **sharper** than any two-edged sword, and piercing as far as the division of soul and spirit, of both joints and marrow, and able to judge the thoughts and intentions of the heart.

Hebrews 4:12

Scripture

References

The scriptures printed in this chapter are referred to in this book.

AFTER EDEN

PAGE 6

Genesis 2:18-24

18   Then the Lord God said, 'It is not good for the man to be alone; I will make him a helper suitable for him.'

19   Out of the ground the Lord God formed every beast of the field and every bird of the sky, and brought them to the man to see what he would call them; and whatever the man called a living creature, that was its name.

20   The man gave names to all the cattle, and to the birds of the sky, and to every beast of the field, but for Adam there was not found a helper suitable for him.

21   So the Lord God caused a deep sleep to fall upon the man, and he slept; then He took one of his ribs and closed up the flesh at that place.

22   The Lord God fashioned into a woman the rib, which He had taken from the man, and brought her to the man.

23   The man said,
'This is now bone of my bones,
And flesh of my flesh;
She shall be called Woman,
Because she was taken out of Man.'

24   For this reason a man shall leave his father and his mother, and be joined to his wife; and they shall become one flesh.

Matthew 19:4-5

4   And He answered and said, 'Have you not read that He who
created them from the beginning MADE THEM MALE AND FEMALE,
5   and said, "FOR THIS REASON A MAN SHALL LEAVE HIS FATHER AND
MOTHER AND BE JOINED TO HIS WIFE, AND THE TWO SHALL BECOME
ONE FLESH"?'

PAGE 7

Genesis 2:16-17

16   The LORD God commanded the man, saying, 'From any tree of
the garden you may eat freely;
17   but from the tree of the knowledge of good and evil you shall
not eat, for in the day that you eat from it you will surely die.'

PAGE 16

Genesis 1:24-31

24   Then God said, 'Let the earth bring forth living creatures
after their kind: cattle and creeping things and beasts of the earth
after their kind'; and it was so.
25   God made the beasts of the earth after their kind, and the
cattle after their kind, and everything that creeps on the ground
after its kind; and God saw that it was good.
26   Then God said, 'Let Us make man in Our image, according to
Our likeness; and let them rule over the fish of the sea and over
the birds of the sky and over the cattle and over all the earth, and
over every creeping thing that creeps on the earth.'
27   God created man in His own image, in the image of God He

created him; male and female He created them.

28   God blessed them; and God said to them, 'Be fruitful and multiply, and fill the earth, and subdue it; and rule over the fish of the sea and over the birds of the sky and over every living thing that moves on the earth.'

29   Then God said, 'Behold, I have given you every plant yielding seed that is on the surface of all the earth, and every tree which has fruit yielding seed; it shall be food for you;

30   and to every beast of the earth and to every bird of the sky and to every thing that moves on the earth which has life, I have given every green plant for food'; and it was so.

31   God saw all that He had made, and behold, it was very good. And there was evening and there was morning, the sixth day.

PAGE 51

Job 40:15-24

15   Behold now, Behemoth, which I made as well as you;
He eats grass like an ox.

16   Behold now, his strength in his loins
And his power in the muscles of his belly.

17   He bends his tail like a cedar;
The sinews of his thighs are knit together.

18   His bones are tubes of bronze;
His limbs are like bars of iron.

19   He is the first of the ways of God;
Let his maker bring near his sword.

20   Surely the mountains bring him food,
       And all the beasts of the field play there.
21   Under the lotus plants he lies down,
       In the covert of the reeds and the marsh.
22   The lotus plants cover him with shade;
       The willows of the brook surround him.
23   If a river rages, he is not alarmed;
       He is confident, though the Jordan rushes to his mouth.
24   Can anyone capture him when he is on watch,
       With barbs can anyone pierce his nose?

PAGE 60

1 Peter 1:24-25
   24   For,
     'ALL FLESH IS LIKE GRASS,
     AND ALL ITS GLORY LIKE THE FLOWER OF GRASS.
     THE GRASS WITHERS,
     AND THE FLOWER FALLS OFF,
   25   BUT THE WORD OF THE LORD ENDURES FOREVER.'
And this is the word which was preached to you.

PAGE 80

Genesis 9:15
   15   And I will remember My covenant, which is between Me and
you and every living creature of all flesh; and never again shall the
water become a flood to destroy all flesh.

PAGE 106

Romans 8:6-8
6   For the mind set on the flesh is death, but the mind set on the Spirit is life and peace,
7   because the mind set on the flesh is hostile toward God; for it does not subject itself to the law of God, for it is not even able to do so,
8   and those who are in the flesh cannot please God.

PAGE 144

Matthew 14:13-21
13   Now when Jesus heard about John, He withdrew from there in a boat to a secluded place by Himself; and when the people heard of this, they followed Him on foot from the cities.
14   When He went ashore, He saw a large crowd, and felt compassion for them and healed their sick.
15   When it was evening, the disciples came to Him and said, 'This place is desolate and the hour is already late; so send the crowds away, that they may go into the villages and buy food for themselves.'
16   But Jesus said to them, 'They do not need to go away; you give them something to eat!'
17   They said to Him, 'We have here only five loaves and two fish.'
18   And He said, 'Bring them here to Me.'
19   Ordering the people to sit down on the grass, He took the five loaves and the two fish, and looking up toward heaven, He blessed the food, and breaking the loaves He gave them to the disciples, and the disciples gave them to the crowds,

20   and they all ate and were satisfied. They picked up what was left over of the broken pieces, twelve full baskets.

21   There were about five thousand men who ate, besides women and children.

PAGE 144

Colossians 1:16-17

16   For by Him all things were created, both in the heavens and on earth, visible and invisible, whether thrones or dominions or rulers or authorities—all things have been created through Him and for Him.

17   He is before all things, and in Him all things hold together.

PAGE 148

Romans 3:23

23   For all have sinned and fall short of the glory of God.

Welcome to Life
AFTER EDEN
credits

Lorena Rogers
layout and design

Mike Matthews
text editing

Dan Zordel
production manager

A special thank you to:

Dave Mateer
website design and posting
After Eden cartoons

Frost Smith
web support

Stacia McKeever
for many valuable critiques

Ken Ham
for giving *After Eden* the go-ahead
and for teaching me about Genesis

Marcia Lietha
for your love and support
as I constantly search for
cartoon ideas.
I love you!

THANKS!

Dan Lietha